Bs By Bioluminescent Light

AMY LAURENS

OTHER WORKS

Find other works by the author at www.amylaurens.com

Bs By Bioluminescent Light

INKLET #71

AMY LAURENS

Inkprint PRESS
www.inkprintpress.com

Print ISBN: 978-1-925825-78-7
eBook ISBN: 9798201616359

www.inkprintpress.com

National Library of Australia Cataloguing-in-Publication Data
Laurens, Amy 1985 –
Bs By Bioluminescent Light
58 p.
ISBN: 978-1-925825-78-7
Inkprint Press, Canberra, Australia
1. Fiction—Science Fiction—General 2. Fiction—Short Stories 3. Fiction—Science Fiction—Space Exploration

First Print Edition: December 2021
Cover photo © Khusen Rustamov via Pixabay
Cover design © Inkprint Press
Interior art © Amy Laurens

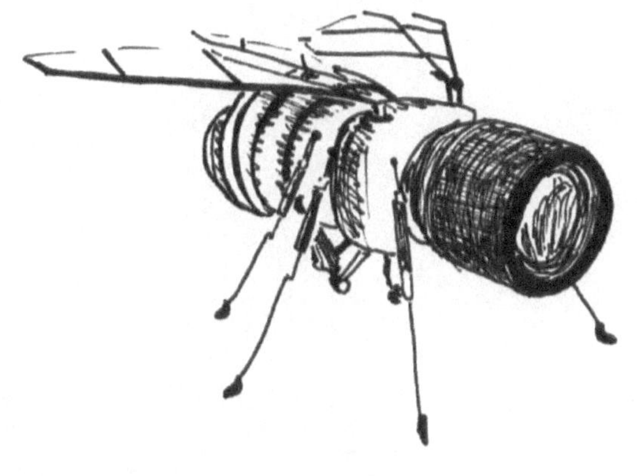

BS BY
BIOLUMINESCENT
LIGHT

SHE SAT ALONE ON A SLATTED PARK bench while the cool night air washed over the exposed skin on her hands, her face. For a moment, she closed her eyes and raised her chin toward it, savouring the freshness, the lingering, indistinct sweetness that the fruit trees gave off after sundown when they'd been baking in the heat all day long. She opened her eyes again, rested her gaze on the slight sliver of twilight, teal and dying blue just glimpsed between the high-rises to the east. The stars above were getting their twinkle on now, and in a moment, the trees that filled the large city park would be too.

She busied herself in the meantime trying to spot constellations around the towering dark forms of the city buildings. Soon the buildings would be glowing, too, but for a while longer, city-sanctioned dark reigned.

There to the west was the Ship, a constellation of five large stars forming the body of a spaceship, with two smaller ones indicating the ship's fins.

Directly above… She smiled. Earth was looking mighty fine tonight. She shifted her tongue, running it along the slight ridgeline around her gum where just weeks ago the dentist had sutured in new teeth. The old set had done nearly nine decades for her. They'd had a good run.

Ah! There! The first of the trees that scattered the park began to glow—the great, spreading branches of the oaks always seemed to light up first, leaves encased a soft, gentle azure.

She shifted her weight on the slatted bench, easing the pain in her bad hip. Sitting in the cooling night was never the best for it, and it was the reason she only sat outside for duskfall weekly now rather than daily—but she wasn't ready to relinquish her miracles just yet.

It didn't help that she had no one to relinquish them *to*.

The glow of the oaks brightened in the dark, enough that she could indistinctly see fallen leaves and a small twig or two littering the grass below.

A sudden movement across the park drew her eye: a small figure, barely more than a silhouette in the dark where the trees' bioluminescence had not kicked in yet—a child.

She watched silently as the child meandered across the park toward her, sometimes darting hither and thither, sometimes stopping for long moments to investigate something of interest.

Reminded her of a hummingdrone, or a B.

That made her smile again.

The row of interplanted apple and plum trees bordering the southern boundary of the park behind her came on; the apple immediately above her waved soft golden leaves that shushed in a sudden lifting of the breeze.

She inhaled deeply, full to the brim with sweet air that seemed to strip the heaviness from her body, even as the cooling temperature stiffened her joints. She flexed her fingers, stretching them out against the niggling pains, rubbed rhythmically at her knuckles.

The child was closer now, eight, twelve metres away and standing close to the trio of birches whose already ghostly trunks were also beginning to join the night-time glow. A girl, her hair—light enough to catch some of the birches' silver glow—pulled back into scruffy, tangled pigtails.

Her lips twitched. She remembered still coming home with hair like that, the way her mother had tugged and combed and teased the knots away, threatening all the while to shave her fair hair clean off like her brother. Her granddaughter must be about this age by now, though it was hard to say, since Kathy hadn't kept in touch.

"What are you doing?" the girl said.

"I'm waiting for something," she replied, then glanced around the empty park, some parts still wreathed in shadows, some gently illuminated by the gradually lightening trees. "Where are your parents?"

The girl shrugged. "Home. I runned away."

She pursed her lips. Yes. That sounded awfully familiar too. "Be so kind as to help me up?" she asked.

"Are you finished waiting?" The girl's voice was light, curious. Nimbly, she darted forward and offered a small, chubby hand. "I'm Tyra. Mama says I'm apposed to tell my name when I meet someone. But not my actual name, just my first one."

Her heart stopped, just for an instant. Tyra. What were the odds? But she took the proffered hand—sticky though it was—and used it to help herself to her feet. She stretched, neck popping, rubbed at her fingers again for momentary relief, pulled a face as she took the first, stiff step.

"Are you sore?" little Tyra piped.

"Always," she said shortly. "But it's no matter. Come on, show me where your parents are."

Tyra hesitated, lip between her teeth, eyes huge like a full moon in the dim light. "Mama says I'm not apposed to tell people where I live."

She nodded solemnly. "You have a very wise Mama. I'll bet Mama said not to run off alone too, didn't she now."

Tyra's face split into an instant grin, and for a moment she outshone the trees. "Yes. But I runned carefully." She puffed up, so proud of her exploits. "I'm not gonna get hurt. I'm very, very careful."

It was so hard not to grin back. "Come," she said. "You don't have to show me where you live, if you'd rather not. But I'd quite like to meet Mama."

Tyra weighed it up for a moment, then shrugged. "This way!" She darted off at a run, not noticing for ten, fifteen steps that her new friend wasn't keeping up. Tyra stopped, pouted. "You walk slow."

She nodded. "I do. It makes me sad,

but it hurts to move much faster when you're my age."

Tyra's brow furrowed. "Will *I* get old?"

Another nod. "Eventually."

Tyra's mouth dropped in an exaggerated O for a moment. She wrinkled her nose. "I don't wanna get old."

"No." She sighed, a fragile, ephemeral thing like a bird flying away. "None of us do."

Tyra stared a moment longer as her new friend closed the gap between them, then reached out and tucked her tiny hand firmly into the larger one. "Your hands are cold."

"Mmm." They were, a little; that's why they were hurting right now—well, not hurting, she allowed, but, kind of... buzzing, tingling, a ghost of the pain to come. Niggling. Ignorable, but enough to stop her doing something like painting.

She missed painting.

They wandered through the park, Tyra compensating for the lack of pace with her high-pitched, rambling conversation, flitting from topic to topic exactly like a hummingdrone between flowers.

Tyra's new friend smiled, pleased that the earlier comparison had proved so apt.

They were about halfway across the park when the lights in the high-rise in front of them came on, a soft blue glow in about three quarters of the windows that indicated occupants going about their evening lives in their homes.

A faint hum drifted on the breeze.

She stopped. Cocked her head. Smiled the smile of someone particularly satisfied.

"What? What is it?" little Tyra asked.

"Listen." She tilted her head in the

direction of the building and widened her eyes, watching in the dim light.

She could hear them; any moment now she'd spot them. Ah! There! "Look," she said simply, pointing to the high-rise above the treeline.

Tyra peered up into the darkness. "I don't see anything."

"Keep watching."

The buzzing hum grew louder. She watched as the small, fragmented cloud poured out of a hole in the building four or five stories up.

Tyra gasped, fingers flying to her mouth. Then she pointed. "Look at it! What is it?"

"Here, I'll show you." She freed her hand and brought her fingers to her mouth. With the assistance of her finger and thumb, she let out a piercing series of whistles, shrill in the quiet of the early night.

Tyra stared up curiously, then stuck her own fingers in her mouth. "Pbbbt.

Pbbbbbbbbt. I can't do it," she added sadly.

She glanced down, offered half a smile. "Maybe I'll teach you. If Mama agrees."

Tyra bounced on the balls of her feet. "When? Can we do it now? Can you teach me now?"

She shook her head, then pointed ahead to where the cloud of dark specks was reaching the stand of oaks. "This is what I was waiting for." The cloud spread, diluting, but handful of specks keyed in on Tyra and her new friend, buzzing closer. "Hold out your hand. No, like this." She demonstrated for Tyra, palm up, nice and flat, fingers flexed and out of the way. "It will tickle, but they won't hurt you, I promise."

Tyra's lip went between her teeth again, her eyes round in the soft light of the trees.

The last of the twilight had faded away now. It must be going on nine o'clock, and Tyra couldn't be more than, what, five, six years old?

"How old are you, Tyra?" she asked.

"Four'na half." Tyra said it confidently, but her gaze was still sweeping the park around them, watching for the mysterious thing that she was holding her hand out for.

Four, good heavens. Mama must be worried sick by now.

Never mind, it wouldn't take a minute or two more to show Tyra the Bs, then she'd deliver her straight back and all would be well.

The specks drew closer—and so did the buzzing noise.

Tyra shrank back.

"There, now, it's okay, they won't hurt you. See?" She held her hand steady as one, two, three little robot pollination drones no bigger than the tip of her pinky landed on her palm, their tiny feet tickling her lifeline, their little wing-propellers buzzing. "Bs, you see?" She offered her palm to Tyra, who tipped her head forward, staring at the little silvered robots as they trod an erratic path, the azure glow of the oaks' bioluminescence reflecting in their bodies.

"Bs," Tyra breathed.

"Put your hand out. I'll call some more."

Obediently, Tyra lifted her hand and waited while her new friend whistled.

Another B buzzed over and landed on Tyra's palm. Tyra flinched, then giggled. "It tickles."

She smiled gently. "It does, doesn't it." One of the Bs gave up on finding pollen on this strange surface it had found and buzzed away into the night. A moment later, the second B joined it. "Never mind," she said. "One for each of us still."

"What's it do?" Tyra asked, gaze fixed on the glimmering B as it wandered over her wrist.

"They pollinate," she said. "Visit flowers," she added at Tyra's puzzled look. "Flowers need something to help them make fruit and vegetables for us. The Bs help."

Tyra grinned, raising her hand close to her nose so the B was level with her eyes. "I like Bs."

"Me too." If she'd thought the breeze was invigorating, carrying as it did the smell of freshness and growing things, it was nothing to this: sharing a treasured moment with someone who loved it just as much as she did. "Did you know there were real bees once?" she said, brimming over at the chance to share her life's passion with an enthusiastic audience.

"Real Bs?"

"Yes, alive ones."

Tyra tilted her head back, eyebrows high, eyes wide. "There were *alive* Bs?"

"Yes. They died though." Back on Earth, before she was even a twinkle in her mother's eye—before her mother had been a twinkle, really. Seventy or so years before the Relocation.

Tyra's brow knitted. "But Bs are good. Why did they die?"

"Ah, well. People forgot that Bs were good, you see. And they…" She sighed, glancing up at the blue glow of the carefully-designed high-rises, buildings full of apartments that were crafted to minimise each human's footprint on the environment, relying on bioluminescence for lighting even though here, on Proxima B, there were no live animals with circadian rhythms to confuse.

"They poisoned the world," she said simply. "Made it so the bees got sick."

Tyra's frown deepened. "But that's

mean. Mama says we should always be careful not to hurt the world."

"Your Mama is a smart woman."

She thought that might be the end of it as Tyra brought the B to her nose again and stared, cross-eyed, as it set off exploring down Tyra's middle finger. But after a moment, Tyra said, "Why didn't they stop the bees from dying?"

She smiled gently. "They didn't realise they were. How many Bs are you used to seeing flying around?" She bobbed her hand slightly to underscore her point.

"None," Tyra answered easily. "I haven't seen a B afore."

"That's right. But my mother, my Mama, she grew up on Earth. So did her mama, my…" She waved her free hand. "What do you call your Mama's mama? Your… Nan? Grandma?"

Tyra shook her head. "My Nan died last year. But I do have a Nanma still!"

She nodded. "Yes, your Nanma, then. Well, my Nanma grew up on Earth, too. She learned about insects, just like *her* mama. Like these Bs, but ones that were alive. And not just bees, but all kinds of insects. Hundreds of them."

"*Hun*dreds?"

She nodded. "Hundreds of different types, and hundreds and hundreds of *each* type. Lots and lots, so many, flying around all the time. Well," she allowed, "not so much in my Nanma's lifetime, that's the point, really. Each of us gets used to the number of insects we see around us and think it's normal. But my great-grandmother studied insects too and she wrote down stories for us, and she says there were hundreds of insects that you could see all the time, even during the day."

Tyra's eyebrows lifted. "Even during the *day*?"

Another solemn nod. "Even during the day."

"*I* wanna go to *Earth*." Tyra's chest puffed up with determination. "I wanna see in-seks."

Devastating, to have to tell her the truth. "Ah, sweetheart. There *are* no more insects on Earth. That's why we flew here in the first place."

"We flew here because the in-seks were gone?"

She nodded. "We hurt the world," she said, borrowing a phrase Tyra was obviously familiar with. "And so it broke. The insects all died out, and it was hard to make enough food for everybody. There were drones, like these Bs"—she bobbed her hand again—"but bigger, more like hummingdrones, and there were so many people with nowhere to live."

Tyra tilted her head. "We hurt the world, so we flew away to find another one?"

In essence. "Yes." It was a miracle that physicists Brooks and Nelson had cracked the mystery of faster-than-light travel when they did. An even bigger miracle that Proxima B, now only two Earth-years away, proved habitable.

Tyra shifted in the night, feet scuffing on the grass. "What did *you* learn about?" she said. "Did you learn about in-seks too?"

Her eyebrows lifted. "Me? Robots. I learned about robots. Drones, mostly."

"Drones. That's why you can talk B language," Tyra said with an emphatic nod.

Despite herself, she laughed. "Yes, that's why I can talk B language." She twisted her bottom lip, considering.

Inhaled.

Stopped.

Exhaled.

It was funny, that this should be such a nerve-wracking confession. But she'd never wanted fame. Had worked hard, in fact, to reclaim her anonymity after fame had ruined her daughter's life, and their relationship.

Silly. What harm could it do now? She shook her head, and bent close to Tyra's blonde one. "Tyra, can you keep a secret?"

"I love secrets!" Tyra twisted toward her, jostling the B on her palm. It flew away—self preservation—and Tyra stared longingly after it.

"Here," she said, tipping her own B onto Tyra's palm, her other hand cupped under Tyra's sticky one to stabilise it. "Have mine. ...That's the secret, actually," she said. She leaned in close, whispering. "The Bs are mine. Or, well, I designed them at least. This version. My Mama designed the first generation of them," she added, straightening. "And the dirt bugs."

"Dirt bugs?" Tyra stared up, curiosity plain on her chubby-cheeked face. "What are dirt bugs?"

"You haven't heard of dirt bugs?!" She blinked, shaking her head. "What in the world are they teaching at school these days."

"I go to Big School this year," Tyra said proudly.

"Well, yes, I suppose you do." That explained her ignorance somewhat, but still. It was practically criminal. Four and a half, and Tyra had never seen a picture of a dirt bug? "Here," she said. "Down here."

It hurt, clambering awkwardly to her knees, and she hissed as pain spiked through her hip.

"What are you doing?"

"Come on." She patted the grass by her side.

Tyra sat dutifully, her B still carefully balanced in one hand.

She leaned over, parting the thick grass, burrowing her fingers in and down. The turf snapped and crackled as the roots broke. She peeled away some of the sod, the dirt below damp and cool. "Bring some leaves," she said.

Carefully, Tyra got to her feet, dashed away, and returned with a twig of silver-glowing birch leaves. "My B flew away," Tyra said, pouting as she dropped to her knees.

"Never mind," she said. "Pass me those leaves." She took them and held them over the dirt, illuminating it. Wait for it, wait for it...

Proxima B had proved habitable, but it had been mostly barren. Water and rock, a decent atmosphere... but nothing live.

And the only life humanity had been able to bring during the Relocation—climate refugees, over a billion of them, it was evacuate or starve and her mother had told her the propaganda was like that of the old, old wars: Do your duty to the Earth! We need YOU! Sign up now to settle the frontier! A better life for everyone!—had been microbes, and thank heavens they'd been able to manage *that*, because it was complicated enough trying to sustain humanity without macro-animal input, let alone trying to even imagine living without microbes.

So it wasn't that the still, quiet soil underneath their knees and currently illuminated in the night by the silver leaves was devoid of life; it was just devoid of *visible* life.

To get around the myriad problems brought on by a lack of fauna—insects in particular—drone technology had quickly advanced. In particular, three main groups had been designed: the Bs, which took care of pollination and associated roles; the leafers, which broke down plant matter and recycled nutrients back to ground level; and the dirt bugs, which lived at varying depths in the soil itself, turning the soil over, processing decaying matter, transporting nutrition, and so forth. It was clumsy, and for several years in the early days barely tenable...

But now, almost ninety years on, the system worked. Well enough to support human life, at any rate. They had crops, they had trees for oxygen, and they had nutrient cycling to maintain the soil.

It was more, perhaps, than anyone could have hoped for when they set off for Proxima B in little more than glorified tin cans.

Tyra squealed.

Hauled back from her reverie, she almost laughed. "Yes, that's a dirt bug."

This particular model—a Slater 965, if she wasn't mistaken—was a segmented, oval-shaped critter a little smaller than the Bs. She squinted, dredging her memory. Dirt bugs had always been her mother's specialty, but probably this was one of the types whose function was the breakdown of organic matter.

Probably.

"It turns dead leaves into dirt so that more trees can grow," she said anyway, because Tyra wouldn't know the difference and the little girl's enthusiasm for the tiny bug trundling across the open stretch of dirt was obvious.

Tyra sighed, a sound of pure contentment. "I *love* dirt bugs."

This time, she did laugh, a short chuckle of delight. "I do too." She leaned sideways a little, close to Tyra. "Though I still like the Bs the best."

Tyra nodded solemnly. "I like the dirt bugs and you like the Bs and that's fair because now they're all liked."

She laughed again. "True enough, little Tyra."

Never mind about the leafers. She grinned to herself. Plenty of people left over to love the leafers.

Abruptly, she realised that Earth had rotated a noticeable way across the night sky. "Oh, Tyra. Quick, quick, get up, help me up, your mama's going to be worried sick about you." She patted the grass back down in place and cast the birch leaves aside, their silver glow already waning now they'd been plucked from their tree.

Tyra stood patiently while her new friend leaned heavily on her shoulder to regain her feet, but she frowned. "Am I gonna get in trouble?"

"Quick, come on now, let's just hurry the best we can." They joined hands again and hurried—at least as fast as someone with a dicky hip could hurry—across the remainder of the park.

They reached the iron gate that marked one of the entrances, went through, let it clang shut behind them. The noise echoed in the quiet night.

"Which one is your apartment?" she said.

"That one." Tyra pointed at the building on the northern edge of the park, one row back from the one that had been among the first to light up after true dark fell.

They hurried along the manicured gravel path that edged the road, footsteps crunch-crunch-crunching as though they were alone in the world. The entrance to the building was around the other side, facing a different park, and by the time they stopped at the double glass doors of the high-rise, her hip was throbbing. She didn't mind over much; she'd have to use a heat pack to get to sleep tonight, take it easy the next day or two, but it would pass. She wouldn't trade her adventures with Tyra for anything.

They paused in front of the keypad that controlled the front doors.

"Do you know your number?" she asked.

Tyra shook herself loose. "Of course! I live in house three three zero three!" She stood on tiptoes to press the keys, over-firm as she lined her finger up and leaned against each one.

A bell rang, then a woman, sounding harried, answered. "Yes, hello?"

"Hi, Mama!" Tyra said brightly.

"Tyra Louise, where in the world have you been? I'm opening the door and you had better get your butt up here now, your father's been searching the park for an hour."

"I was in the *other* park," Tyra piped. "I made a friend!"

"A friend?" Mama's voice turned sharp.

She coughed, politely. "Um, hello. I found your daughter wandering in Sibylla Merian Park. I've brought her back?" Straight away. Definitely did not spend too much time dallying over tiny robots and insect-replacement drones.

"I see." The sharpness had dropped away from Mama's voice; instead, suspicion layered thick over it. "Well, come up, please."

They did. The elevator took its time, but Tyra chattered away, talking about the Bs and dirt bug they'd seen, telling her about the bear Nanma had gifted Tyra as a birthday present, about the party Mama was throwing on the weekend—"It's a surprise," Tyra said very seriously. "I'm going to stay in my room and they are gonna put gretchens up and balloons and then I'll come out and they'll all shout SURPRISE and there's gonna be *cake*."—and fifty other things besides.

It took her a moment, but by the time Tyra had cycled through at least two more topics, she said, "Oh, gretchens. Do you mean decorations?"

Tyra nodded. "Yes. Gretchens."

The elevator dinged.

"This way!" Tyra dashed ahead. She paused at the corner of a hallway carpeted in navy blue, a deeper shade of the same colour the white walls were presently glowing due to the fan-shaped bio-lights set into them.

She smiled. It was a very nice apartment block, no stains on the walls, the carpet thick and soft beneath her tread. Her chest felt light again; briefly she wondered at the fact that this small blonde child whom she'd only met an hour or so ago had suddenly come to mean so much to her.

Ah well. That's what happened when you got old and lonely, she thought with a large dose of self-deprecation.

"*Come* on," Tyra said.

She smiled wryly and followed Tyra down the warm hall, past a door on the right that failed to contain tantalising smells of something mex-spiced, a door on the left that stood slightly ajar, the sound of either a high-action movie or else a very intense break-in radiating out—and they arrived at 3303.

Tyra banged on the door. "Mama!!" she sang out. "I'm hoo-oome."

The door opened and a plump, dark-haired woman just this side of middle age swept Tyra up into her arms, the hem of her red shirt puckering above the waistband of her jeans, exposing a flash of pale skin.

"Tyra Louise, don't you *ever* go wandering like that again."

"Yes, Mama," Tyra said in a small voice, burying her head against her mother's shoulder.

"Good," Mama said firmly, putting Tyra back on the floor. "Now go clean your teeth, it's so far past your bed-time you're going to turn into a B."

"I saw a B!" Tyra peeped.

"Did you now. Go clean your teeth. You can tell me tomorrow." Mama shooed Tyra into the house, stared after her for a moment, and turned back with a shake of her head. "Thank you," Mama said. "For bringing her back. I swear, I don't know what I'm going to do with her some days. She just *wanders*, always because she had questions about something or other and wanted to find out the answers for herself." Mama shook her head.

On the doorstep, Tyra's new friend hesitated. "Your daughter…" she said. "She's very bright. I know she's about to start school, but… maybe… Do you think if she had some extra tutoring that might help channel her curiosity?"

Why was her heart pounding like this? How ridiculous. *Stop being stupid,* she told herself firmly.

She caught the suspicion lingering in Mama's eye. "I have credentials," she added. "I used to teach at the university. My child safety checks are still up to date and everything."

Mama pursed her lips.

"Please, Mama?" As though from thin air, Tyra reappeared, clinging to her mother's arm. "Please can I learn about the Bs? And the dirt bugs? And in-seks?"

"Dirt bugs!" Mama hesitated, gaze flickering from Tyra to her friend and back again. Then, all at once, she sighed, the tension leaving her shoulders, her neck. "Alright. But only," she added, bending down with her forehead close to Tyra's, "during the day time."

"But Mama, Bs only come out at night! Silly Mama." Tyra shook her head.

Mama's lips pinched in a very familiar way as she stifled a smile. "That's true. You're right. But you're only four."

"Nearly five!"

Mama nodded. "Yes, I know, nearly five. Okay, well. How about only on weekends? Once a week," she queried, glancing up at Tyra's friend. "Would that work?"

She nodded gravely, though her heart was beating like it would palpate right out of her chest. "Alphday's best for me."

Another decisive nod. "Alphday. Does it have to be this late?"

She offered an apologetic smile. "I'm afraid the drones don't come out until late this time of year."

It had been a long time since she'd wanted something this much.

And she was terrified to show it, in case Mama misread her intentions.

"*Please*, Mama? Pleeeeaaase?" Tyra tugged on Mama's arm.

"Yes, *fine*," Mama said, sighing the word explosively. "Alphday," she said. "At eight." She detached Tyra from her arm, shooed her back into the depths of her house, and stared. "I suppose you'd better come in," she said at last. "If you're going to be Tyra's tutor and all. What's your name?" Mama said, stepping back, welcoming Tyra's friend into their home.

It smelled of vanilla, and it clogged her throat with memories of her own Mama. Oh, how much she had missed having a place to go, a place where other people knew her, welcomed her, wanted her. "Tyra," she said as she crossed the threshold. "My name is also Tyra."

Little Tyra appeared again with a squeal. "There are two Tyras! Did you hear that, Mama? Two Tyras!"

Mama nodded, bemused. "Yes, it seems there are."

"And big Tyra is going to teach me all about Bs and dirt bugs and when I grow up, I'm going to be just like her!" Little Tyra puffed up again like the white birds with the yellow crests that were part of the National Bird Memorial Museum's logo. "Except," Tyra added as she tripped away, presumably to the bathroom and her toothbrush, "I'm not going to be *old*."

Mama snorted wryly. "Sorry," she said, cutting a glance at the adult Tyra.

Adult Tyra smiled broadly. "It's fine," she said. "I *am* old, after all."

Old, but no longer alone. Perhaps she didn't have to give up on her miracles just yet after all.

THE MAKING OF
BS BY
BIOLUMINESCENT
LIGHT

This story must nearly win the prize, I think, for the shortest time between writing and publication as an Inklet. In January of 2020, I took an online science fiction writing course. It was fantastic, I had to write three short stories in the space of a week, and my brain nearly exploded from everything I learned—not least of which was that I was *capable* of writing three short stories in a week.

For this particular story, I was tasked with writing something set not on Earth, that in some way spring-boarded from an article in the collection of non-fiction science writing that had been part of the reading list for the course. One of the articles was about the (sad) decline in insect numbers over the last several decades. I didn't think too much about it beyond the fact that that was the article I wanted to leap from, and this story simply unspooled.

I took particular pleasure in writing Little Tyra's dialogue, because she is about the same age my daughter was when I wrote this. For the sake of research, accuracy and the fun of it, I did actually turn to my daughter while writing and say, "Hey kid, do you realise you'll get old someday?"

Tyra's response is my daughter's, almost verbatim.

Read more by Amy Laurens!

CRYSTALLINE AND BRIGHT

I stood, staring down into the teal-blue river water, ignoring the chatter behind my back. The snow covered the ground around me, hiding bumps and ridges, soothing out sharp edges. To my right, the dark stone shadow of the bridge stood like a guardian, watchful, alert. Snow rimmed its edges; every so often some shifted in a sudden breeze and landed in the quiet river below with a gentle splash.

The willows on the far bank slept quietly under their snow blanket, their green sappy smell hidden by the cold, sharp scent of the snow.

Stop.

Start again.

It wasn't actually winter. It was early spring, with the grass green and new, the sound of a lawnmower buzzing in the distance and the scent of cut grass drifting on the wind. Moss covered the shadowed side of the old stone bridge, and willows stretched their fingers to the slow-moving, drowsy little river that bordered the grounds of the school.

A butterfly flittered past, white wings speckled with black like soot.

The world felt fresh, and green, and full of promise.

I was still ignoring the chattering behind me.

Stop.

Start again.

It's summer, and the air is swelteringly hot. Sweat drips down the back of my neck, pools under my arms, under my awkward breasts. The river in front of me is milky-blue, gentle, quiet, and I long to strip off my shirt and jeans and throw myself into the water.

It's not just the breathtakingly sharp cold of the icemelt I'm craving; it's the feeling of being *clean.*

The air stinks of a fish that Lander left out on the bank near the bridge, rotting to pieces in the high temperatures.

I'm still ignoring the chatter.

Stop.

Let's try once more.

It's autumn—of course—and the willows have turned yellow, their little leaves dropping into the milk-water, eddying slowly away from the shadow of the bridge.

Behind me, the emerald lawn of the old school buildings is ringed with gem-toned maples, butter-leafed poplars, silver-and-gold birches. Occasionally, the wind catches stray leaves and flings them into the pond.

I can still hear the voices behind me.

All of these pictures are true, and none of them are.

Not precisely, not uniquely; they're all composites, the merging and piecing together of hundreds of memories of similar experiences, of all the times I stood on the river bank and stared longingly into its depths, imagining myself a naiad with a secret home to return to, somewhere people loved me.

These images have to be composites, because for every time I was down at the river, I was focusing only on two things: ignoring the voices, and watching the water.

All the other details, the little bits of specificity that allow me to recall the place in so much explicit detail? I never noticed them at the time.

And so I have to piece them together, collage-fashion, or else I have nothing to say. Nothing to see.

Nothing except the water, milky-blue that occasionally, in the right light, at the right time of day, flashed teal and came alive.

I'd lived with the voices as long as I could remember. Some of them were real, inasmuch as they belonged to real, live people whom other people could see, who grew and developed and changed with the passing of the seasons; some of them were *surreal*, inasmuch as they belonged to people I could see, but that none other could, and who did not change or grow with the passing of the seasons.

And some of the voices… Some of them I could never divine exactly what they were.

But all of them, real, surreal and unknown, had one thing in common: none of them liked me.

I could never figure out why. Oh, sure, I came to the school without the name and pedigree of any of the other students, a supposed-orphan with no memory of her life before double digits and no connections to speak of. I wasn't part of their circle, my excellent trust fund notwithstanding, and so the real people, the live people, couldn't accept me.

It shouldn't have been that way. It seemed to me that I hadn't done anything wrong, or untoward, hadn't neglected to do anything needed, hadn't slighted or snubbed any who hadn't already done so several times to me.

And yet, for all the years I was there at the school, its grand, lofty double-storey buildings made from pale stone like a castle, ivy creeping all about like Christmas lights, the lawn constantly emerald, the hedges consistently clipped… For all those composite years, no one ever liked me.

Well, a slight exaggeration: my teachers liked me well enough. I was a diligent student.

And the river liked me. I could tell that, because when I was close to the river, the other voices kept their distance—and the river had a voice of its own. And once or twice, I could have sworn it also had a face.

Keep reading! Head to www.inkprintpress.com/ amylaurens/aprilshowers/ to buy your copy now!

ABOUT THE AUTHOR

AMY LAURENS is an Australian author of fantasy fiction for all ages. One day, she will have real bees of her own to tend, but in the meantime, she contents herself with writing about them.

Amy has also written the award-winning portal-fantasy *Sanctuary* series about Edge, a 13-year-old girl forced to move to a small country town because of witness protection (the first book is *Where Shadows Rise*), the humorous fantasy *Kaditeos* series, following newly graduated Evil Overlord Mercury as she attempts to acquire a castle, the young adult series *Storm Foxes*, about love and magic and family in small town Australia, and a whole host of non-fiction.

INKLETS

Collect them all! Released on the 1st and 15th of each month.

INKLET #055
Allure
AMY LAURENS

INKLET #056
The LIES We KNOW
LIANA BROOKS

DOUBLE ISSUE
INKLET #057
AFTERMATH & Fool Me Once
AMY LAURENS

INKLET #058
Purity
An Age Of Unicorns Story
AMY LAURENS

INKLET #059
Saved
AMY LAURENS

INKLET #060
A Kiss is the Secret
AMY LAURENS

INKLET #061
A Changing Tides Story
Fire Bright
AMY LAURENS

INKLET #062
Hades AND Persephone
LIANA BROOKS

INKLET #063
Just So Long As You're Happy
AMY LAURENS

INKLET #064
Theft Of A Lifetime
LIANA BROOKS

INKLET #065
Shoe
AMY LAURENS

INKLET #066
Published AUTHOR
LIANA BROOKS

DOUBLE ISSUE
INKLET #067
THE REMARKABLE INSIGHT OF JELLYBEANS, & Understanding
AMY LAURENS

INKLET #068
Desperate Measures
AMY LAURENS

INKLET #069
Rock-a-bye
LIANA BROOKS

INKLET #070
the Other Carly
AMY LAURENS

INKLET #071
By By Bioluminescent Light
AMY LAURENS

INKLET #072
Even Villains Grant Wishes
A Heroes & Villains Story
LIANA BROOKS